Library of Congress Cataloging-in-Publication Data
Rosenthal, Amy Krouse.
  Uni the unicorn / by Amy Krouse Rosenthal;
  illustrated by Brigette Barrager.
    pages cm.
  Summary: Uni the unicorn believes that little girls are real.
    ISBN 978-0-385-37555-9 (trade) — ISBN 978-0-375-97206-5 (lib. bdg.) —
    ISBN 978-0-375-98208-8 (ebook)
    [1. Unicorns—Fiction.] I. Barrager, Brigette, illustrator. II. Title.
    PZ7.R719445Un 2013 [E]—dc23 2013009884

        ISBN 978-0-593-30622-2 (book & toy set)

        MANUFACTURED IN CHINA
        10 9 8 7 6 5 4 3 2 1

        Book design by John Sazaklis

For my daughter Paris,
a strong smart wonderful magical girl
—A.K.R.

To Sean and Kirsten, for believing in me
—B.B.

Random House 🏠 New York

Amy Krouse Rosenthal

Uni the UNICORN

illustrated by Brigette Barrager

In almost every way,
Uni was like all the other unicorns.

Magnificent mane
(though Uni's was *extra* magnificent).

Golden hooves
(though Uni's were *extra* golden).

Sparkling purple eyes
(though Uni's were *extra* sparkling).

Like the other unicorns,
   Uni had a special swirly horn
   with the power to heal and mend.

And like the
other unicorns,

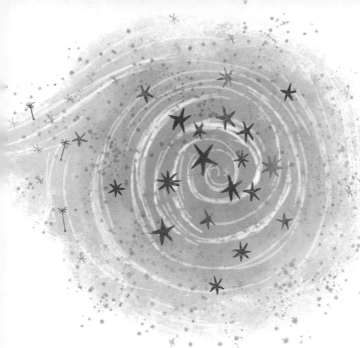

Uni could make wishes come true.

But there was one thing
that definitely set Uni apart. . . .

Uni believed that little girls were REAL.

Uni's friends laughed and said,
"Ha, ha, ha, silly Uni. Everyone knows
there's no such thing as little girls!
They're just make-believe!"

At home, Uni's parents
just brushed it off
with knowing smiles.

But Uni was certain, absolutely certain,
that little girls were real,
no matter what everyone else said.

Uni knew that somewhere far away
(but not *that* far away),
there was a little girl waiting ...
a strong smart wonderful magical little girl.

And she would be the best friend
a unicorn could ever ask for.

Uni imagined all the things
they would do together....

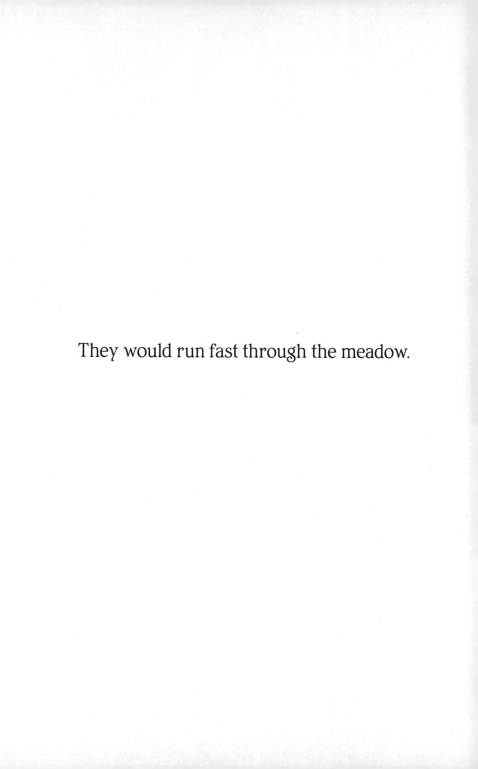

They would run fast through the meadow.

They would spin and twirl in the sunlight.

They would explore, and help
forest creatures in need.

Other times, they would just sit quietly
and talk about important things.

And of course of course of course

they would slide down rainbows together.

Uni fell asleep that night
and had enchanted dreams.

What Uni did not yet know,
   but would discover soon enough,
   was that somewhere far away
   (but not *that* far away) . . .

         . . . there was indeed a real little girl.

And even though her friends said,
"Ha, ha, ha. Unicorns are just
make-believe!"

And despite her parents' knowing smiles...

...this little girl was certain, absolutely certain,
   that there was a unicorn,
      a strong smart wonderful magical unicorn...

. . . just waiting to be her friend.